THE PUPPY

LILY

THE PUPPY PLACE

Don't miss any of these other stories by Ellen Miles!

THE PUPPY PLACE

LILY

ELLEN MILES

SCHOLASTIC INC.

ISBN 978-1-338-68698-2

10 9 8 7 6 5 4 3 2 1   21 22 23 24 25

Printed in the U.S.A.   40
First printing 2021

33614082284190

CHAPTER ONE

"Can we open the windows?" Charles asked.

"Good idea," said Mom. Soon, a rush of fresh air filled the car.

Charles Peterson and his family had been in the car all day. Actually, longer. They had left in the middle of the night. Charles had been asleep, in his pj's, when Dad carried him out to the car. He must have woken up a little bit, because he remembered that it had been cold and dark.

The Petersons had stopped a couple of times on the drive. It had been a little sunnier and a little warmer each time. That was because they were headed south. They were on their way to the beach for spring break, and Charles couldn't wait to get there.

Now it was almost dinnertime, and they had made it all the way to North Carolina. Here, with the sun beating down, it almost felt like they'd skipped spring and gone straight to summer. With the windows open, Charles could smell freshly cut grass and sunbaked dirt. He took a big whiff, smiling. The smell reminded him of summer softball games.

"Windy!" the Bean squealed from his car seat. The Bean's shaggy bangs whipped around his head. The Bean was Charles's little brother, and he needed a haircut.

"It *is* windy, isn't it?" Mom repeated.

Charles looked at his sister, Lizzie. She smiled and rolled her eyes. Mom always repeated what the Bean said. Charles and Lizzie thought it was funny.

"It's windy," Lizzie agreed. "But it's warm. I can't wait to get to Brisco Beach."

The Petersons had been to Brisco Beach once before. It was so much fun! The town was on a narrow stretch of land that reached out into the ocean. One side had waves—big enough for boogie boarding and surfing. On the other side, the bay side, the water was smooth and calm—good for fishing and swimming. Plus, there was a down-town where you could get all kinds of treats and souvenirs. There was even a ferry to the main-land, where there were tons of other fun things to do. Charles had never done that, and he was hoping to go this year.

"The best part of our last trip was Liberty," Lizzie said. "She was the sweetest puppy."

Dad laughed. "You say that about every puppy," he said.

"But it's true," Lizzie said. "They are all the best."

Charles nodded in agreement. "Lizzie's right," he said. His family fostered puppies. They took care of puppies who needed homes, and they worked to find each puppy its forever family. They loved all the puppies they had helped. Of course, one puppy really had been the very, very best, and that puppy had become the Petersons' own puppy—Buddy.

"I still wish Buddy could have come with us," Charles said now, thinking about how much he'd like to stroke the white heart-shaped spot on Buddy's brown chest. Buddy loved that.

Mom turned around in her seat so she could see Charles. "We talked about this. Buddy will have lots of fun with Aunt Amanda."

Aunt Amanda ran a doggy day care. When the Petersons went away, they let Buddy stay with her. Buddy loved playing with the other dogs. Charles knew it was a treat for Buddy, but he also knew he would really miss his favorite puppy. He would miss petting him, and playing with him, and lying on the couch with him. He would miss—well, everything.

"Besides, we're staying at a bed-and-breakfast this year," Mom said. "It's not like we're renting our own place where Buddy would feel at home."

"But we'll get good breakfasts, right?" Lizzie added. "Like pancakes and muffins?"

"Yes," Mom said. "And we can get takeout for dinner. It's a real vacation when Dad and I don't have to cook. It gives us more time to be with you."

Dad nodded. "We're going to teach the Bean how to swim."

"Like a dolphin," the Bean said. He scrunched his lips together, making a fish face.

"That's right, like a dolphin," Mom repeated.

Charles rolled his eyes and grinned at Lizzie. Mom had done it again.

Lizzie smiled, but only for a second. Then she looked back down at the very thick book in her lap. It was the first in a series of very big books, and she had brought them all, saying it was her vacation goal to finish the whole series.

Charles sighed and gazed out the window. He had left his books at home—by mistake. All kinds of books: graphic novels, a book on airplanes, a bunch of mysteries. He had been too asleep when his dad took him to the car, or he would have remembered to grab the extra duffel they were in. He hoped he wouldn't be bored in Brisco Beach.

They had been on the highway for a long time. They'd driven on giant, traffic-filled highways, up and down mountains, and along wide tree-lined roads. But now the view out the window was different. The sky was bright blue, with the hint of a rosy-gold sunset ahead. The air smelled different, too. It was warm and salty and—Charles sniffed—kind of fishy, in a good way.

"Are we close?" Charles asked.

"Very close," Mom said, looking at the directions on her phone.

Charles glanced over at Lizzie. She was still staring at her book. She had her finger resting on the top corner, ready to turn the page. She didn't care about anything but her book.

When they finally pulled into the driveway of the bed-and-breakfast, Charles couldn't wait to get out of the car. He hopped out, stretched, and took a look around. FAIR HARBOR INN said a sign out front. The house looked really old. It was three stories tall, with a porch that wrapped all the way around the front and sides. On the corners of the second and third floors, there were round towers with windows. The windows all had lacy curtains. Charles saw one twitch, and he shivered. There was something spooky about this house. Could it be—haunted?

As Charles stretched some more, waiting for everyone else to get out of the car, a family appeared on the porch. He saw a mom and dad with three little kids—and the cutest cream-colored puppy, a pudgy little thing with soft, wavy hair and floppy ears, and huge chocolate-colored eyes, and—

"Hey!" The oldest kid was holding the puppy's leash—or at least he had been, until the puppy spotted Charles. In a flash, the puppy ran right between the dad's legs and darted down the steps.

Charles knew what to do. He bent down and opened his arms wide. "Come here, pup! Come on!" he called. In seconds, the puppy was in his arms, covering his face in happy puppy kisses.

CHAPTER TWO

"We are so sorry," the mom said, rushing forward. She grabbed the puppy's leash from the ground. "Lily, stop that," she said. Her bracelets jangled as she pulled on the leash. "Lily, you need to stop."

"It's okay," Charles said, laughing. The puppy had her front paws on his chest.

He scratched her behind the ears. "I don't mind. She's really sweet." The puppy licked his chin again, wagging her tail so hard that her whole body wriggled.

Hi, hi, hi! I love new friends. Let's be friends. Let's play!

"She *is* sweet. Especially when she's sleeping," the woman said.

"The rest of the time she's a handful," the dad said with a laugh. "Lily obviously needs an obedience class." Charles had a feeling the man didn't really think it was so funny.

"A good class can make a big difference," Lizzie said. She came around from her side of the car. "She's a golden retriever, right?"

The mom nodded. "She's the kind they call English cream, because of her coloring."

Lizzie nodded. "Goldens are smart and super eager to please," she said. "I think Lily would do really well in a class."

Lizzie knew a lot about dogs. She was even sometimes a bit of a know-it-all, but Charles thought she was right about this puppy. Lily was young and full of energy. Still, Charles could tell she was a good dog. Or at least, she wanted to be.

The three kids raced down from the porch toward Lily. They crowded around Charles. "Lily! Lily! Lily!" they yelled. Six hands reached out for the puppy, who was huddled in Charles's lap. Lily started to bark. They were happy, playful barks. And loud. Very loud.

"Layla, Miles, Benji, take it easy," their mom said. "Remember, she's just a puppy."

Charles saw Benji—the oldest boy, roll his eyes. He had a feeling that Benji had heard that phrase a lot lately. Charles felt a hand on his shoulder. "Charles," his mom said, "we should let the puppy be with her family."

"We're actually headed downtown," said the mom. "Lily needs as many walks as we can give her. Every day." She sounded tired.

Charles lifted Lily out of his lap and placed her on the ground. The puppy barked and barked and barked some more. "It was really nice meeting you," Charles called, over Lily's yips. He smiled at the puppy and waved at the family.

Lily's family waved back as they headed toward town. Lily was in the lead, practically dragging the mom down the sidewalk. At least she wasn't barking anymore!

Charles joined his family on the porch of the bed-and-breakfast, just as a woman with short red hair came to the door. "Come in, come in," she said, motioning with her hand. "Welcome to Fair Harbor Inn. I'm Jodi."

Jodi explained that the inn had once belonged to her grandparents. "My kids and I took over about a year ago. Things have been extra busy since my oldest son, Jeremy, left for college. My youngest, Sophie, is ten—maybe about your age?" She smiled at Lizzie. "And Milo is thirteen."

As Mom and Dad chatted with Jodi, Charles looked out the window. Even though it was starting to get dark, Charles could just make out Lily and her family, way down the sidewalk. Lily was still out in front. That puppy liked to take charge!

"Hello, Earth to Charles!" His dad waved a hand in front of his face, trying to get his attention. "It's time to go upstairs. Grab your bag."

Charles peered down the street, watching Lily prance in front of her family. She really was adorable.

"Sorry, Jodi," Mom said. "I think he's a little distracted by that puppy."

Now, Jodi sighed. "Understandable. That's one cute puppy. One cute puppy who is also a huge troublemaker. We really don't allow dogs here, but they just sort of—showed up with her. What could I do?"

"How is she a troublemaker?" Lizzie asked.

"For one," Jodi said, "she peed on my grandmother's antique quilt."

"What's an antique quilt?" Charles asked.

"It's like a blanket that has been patched together," Mom explained. "And something that is antique is really old. Some of them are very valuable."

Charles nodded. He could understand why Jodi was upset. Charles knew puppies could be hard work. They had a lot of learning to do. And when they acted out, it was especially annoying if the puppy was not your puppy.

"That's not all," Jodi said. She held up her hand and ticked off fingers as she listed Lily's misdeeds. "She chewed on the legs of a bed and on a lamp cord. She ripped a hole in a couch pillow. And she ate something weird and then threw it up on the parlor rug."

A girl who looked a lot like Jodi came from the back of the house. "Plus she barks a lot," she said.

"We heard some of that," Mom said.

14

"It's impossible not to," the girl added. "Late at night. First thing in the morning. The dog barks *a lot*."

"This is Sophie, my daughter," Jodi said.

"Hi," Sophie said with a cheery wave. Her eyes opened wide and she pointed at Lizzie. "I'm reading that book, too! Isn't it the best?"

Lizzie's whole face lit up as she hugged the thick book to her chest. "Yes!"

Charles followed his parents and Jodi upstairs, but Lizzie stayed on the first floor, joining Sophie on the parlor couch. Their faces were almost touching as they discussed the book.

Now that Charles was inside the inn, he still felt that "sorta-maybe-kinda-haunted" feeling. The wooden floors creaked. Ancient brown-and-white photos of frowning men in tall hats and serious women in long skirts lined the walls, and the dim light above the staircase flickered on and off.

"You and Lizzie are in this room," Jodi said, at the top of the stairs. She pointed to the right, to a door with a sign that read MAPLE. "Your mom and dad and little brother will all be right next door, and there's a door connecting the rooms, too." She pointed to another door, to the left. That one's sign said OAK.

"Really?" Charles asked, peeking inside. Wait till Lizzie saw that they were going to stay in one of the rooms with the cool round tower in the corner, and windows on all sides.

The Petersons went to get pizza for dinner. As they walked back to the inn, Charles took a good look at the old place. There were lights on in some of the rooms, and he could see people moving behind the lacy curtains. Under the pale moonlight, Fair Harbor Inn looked spookier than ever.

CHAPTER THREE

Lizzie was right. The breakfast at the Fair Harbor Inn was delicious—and there was plenty of it. Charles had two eggs, plus seconds on pancakes and thirds on bacon.

"Jodi, these muffins are amazing," Mom said.

"Thanks," Jodi replied. She set a mug of hot chocolate next to Lizzie's plate. "That's nice to hear."

"Running this inn has to be a lot of work," Mom said. "And you have three kids, too!"

"Well, my oldest son, Jeremy, was a huge help before he left for college," Jodi said. "Sophie helps some in the kitchen. But lately Milo spends all his time in his room." Jodi paused for a moment. Then she added, "Video games!" making a "yuck" face.

"Well, we won't be in our rooms today. We're going to the bay side of the beach today," Mom said. "The Bean needs some swim practice. What about you, Lizzie and Charles?"

Lizzie held up the book that sat next to her plate. "Sophie and I are going to read on the porch," she said.

Charles could tell that Lizzie and Sophie had become instant friends. He wished he had a new friend, too. "Has the family with the puppy come down yet?" he asked Jodi. He remembered that the oldest boy, Benji, seemed close to his age. Plus, there was Lily! He could play with that puppy all day.

"You know, they checked out early," said Jodi. "I didn't even hear them leave, but I found their key on the breakfast table when I came out to set it."

Charles frowned. He thought he had heard the puppy that morning. He definitely had heard her bark overnight.

"It was a little weird. I didn't think they were leaving until tomorrow," Jodi said as she put a bowl of fruit down on the table. "They were paid up for another day."

"Maybe they had some sort of family emergency," Mom said. She reached for another muffin. For the next several minutes, the only sound was the scrape of forks on plates.

As soon as they were done eating, Mom and Dad announced they were taking the Bean to the bay. "We'll be there until lunch," Dad said. "How about you two?"

Charles was glad that Mom and Dad let him and Lizzie go to the beach on their own. Brisco Beach was a super-safe place. Charles and Lizzie knew that there were rules to follow about not swimming without an adult present and about checking in regularly.

"Until lunch? I'll come, but I want to bring the pail and shovel," said Charles. Charles liked to swim, but he really liked to boogie-board in the waves on the ocean side. The bay side did not have any waves. The water was smooth. If Charles had a pail and shovel, he could build a sandcastle, or search for hermit crabs, or bury his dad in the sand.

"Good idea," Mom said. "They're in the big bag in our room." She gave him the key.

Charles ran up the creaky stairs. As he reached for the doorknob of his parents' room, he heard something. It sounded like a high-pitched moan. He stopped to look around, but he was the only one in the hallway. He heard the sound again, and felt goose bumps up his arms and a tingling at the back of his neck. The lace curtain in the window at the end of the hall swayed, as if someone had just walked by. Charles squinted his eyes and shook his head. This house was just downright spooky, even during the day. Everything was brighter, but there were still those brown-and-white photos of very serious people on the walls. Charles had felt like their eyes were following him as he climbed the stairs.

He took a deep breath, turned the key in the lock, and pushed open the door.

The room looked the same as it had when he'd seen it that morning. He rushed over to the big bag with all the beach toys. It was by the open window. When he leaned down, he felt a breeze come in from outside. Then, as he was searching, he thought he heard that eerie, high moaning sound again. The goose bumps popped up on his arms as Charles glanced around the room and out the window. He almost felt those spooky eyes on him again. The second his hand found his shovel and pail, he rushed for the door.

He gave the room one last peek, and then closed the door and put the key in the lock. For a moment, he looked at the door to the room right next to Mom and Dad's, on the other side. Was the sound coming from there? Was that room . . . haunted? Was that why the other family had left early?

Charles took a step toward the door, which had a sign saying SYCAMORE. He took another step, and the floorboard squeaked. Charles jumped.

Then the thundering sound of footsteps filled the hallway as someone came barreling down the stairs, right at him. Charles yelped.

"Oh, hey!" said a boy with long, curly bangs. He came to a stop in front of Charles and shook back his hair. "I'm Milo. I live here." He motioned upstairs. "Up there, on the third floor." Milo was tall and very skinny.

"I'm Charles. I'm staying here." Charles motioned to the door. "In the Maple room."

Milo nodded. "Good thing you aren't in Sycamore," he said with a grin. "It's haunted."

Charles gulped. He blinked several times.

Milo laughed and gave Charles's shoulder a little shove. "Just kidding," he said. "See you around."

Milo brushed past him and barreled down the next flight of stairs. Charles couldn't move. He looked at the door of Sycamore again. He listened, but he didn't hear anything.

Maybe he'd just been imagining things.

Maybe it was time to go build a sandcastle.

CHAPTER FOUR

While he was at the beach, Charles totally forgot about the spooky sounds at the inn. He swam and splashed with Dad. He searched for shells and sea glass. He built a sandcastle with the Bean. Or rather, he built a lot of sandcastles, and the Bean knocked every one of them down.

Soon, Charles was ready for another swim. "Can I go back to the inn?" he asked. "I forgot my swim mask."

"Of course," Dad said. "The keys are in Mom's beach bag. You know the way, right?"

Charles nodded. The inn was only five minutes from the bay. The path, a wooden boardwalk, went through dunes covered with marsh grasses. The grass was as tall as Charles, and it swayed and rustled in the wind. Charles listened to his flip-flops slapping on the sun-warmed wooden planks and took deep breaths of the salty air. He was happy to be back in Brisco Beach.

In the sunlight, Fair Harbor Inn actually looked cheery and bright. Charles ran up the porch steps, through the front door, and up the stairs. As he searched for the key in the pocket of his swim shorts, he heard that strange moaning noise again. He stopped and listened. "Hello?" he said. After a deep breath he took a step toward the door of the Sycamore room. "Hello?" Charles knocked on the door. If there was a ghost in there, would it answer back?

The moaning stopped. Then a loud bark rang out. And another.

Charles recognized that bark. It had to be Lily,

the adorable puppy from yesterday. "Lily, is that you?" Charles called out. He grabbed the door-knob and tried to twist it open, but it was locked. He leaned up against the door. "Hang on, Lily," he called. "I'm going to get help."

Charles raced down the stairs. His flip-flops slapped against his feet. "Jodi! Jodi!" he yelled. "Jodi! I need your help." Charles flew into the dining room, peeked into the kitchen, and ran out onto the porch. He called for Jodi everywhere he went, but there was no answer, and no sign of her anywhere. Then he remembered Milo. Jodi had said that Milo was almost always in his room.

Charles dashed all the way to the third floor, taking the stairs two at a time. "Milo!" he said at the top of the stairs. "Milo?" he called again, panting. The door at the end of the hallway was slightly open. Charles ran to it and looked inside.

Milo was sitting at a desk with his back to the door, staring at a computer. The headphones he wore explained why he hadn't heard Charles.

"Milo!" Charles said his name loudly, but the older boy did not turn around. Charles walked right into the room and tapped the boy's shoulder.

"Aaaaaah!" Milo jumped and turned to stare at Charles. "What are you doing in here?"

"I'm really sorry," Charles answered with a gulp. "But there's a sound coming from the Sycamore room. I think it's that puppy, Lily!"

Milo's eyebrows shot up, then scrunched together. "What? Are you sure?"

Charles nodded. "Can you unlock the door?" Charles asked. "I can't find your mom."

"Um, yeah," Milo said. He pulled off his headphones and pushed himself away from the desk. "I just need to find the master keys. They're downstairs. Somewhere."

Once Milo stood up, he was in high gear. He took long strides toward the stairs. "Meet me at Sycamore," he called over his shoulder.

Milo thundered down the steps. Charles followed, stopping in front of the Sycamore room.

"Hang in there, Lily," Charles said to the door. "We'll get you out soon." He heard a small squeal in response. Poor Lily.

Milo came tearing back up the stairs. He mumbled to himself as he flipped through the keys on the crowded ring. "Here we go," he said. He slid a key into the lock and turned the knob.

A volley of barks greeted them as soon as they opened the door and stepped inside.

Charles ran to the other side of the room, close to the big window. There was Lily, still locked in her travel crate. The puppy barked again, and then she pawed at the floor of the crate.

*I'm so glad you're here! Let me out! I'm hungry!
And I need to go outside! Get me out of here!*

As soon as Charles had unzipped the carrier, Lily burst out. She ran circles around Charles. Then she ran circles around Milo. She barked and barked and barked.

Both boys knelt down, trying to calm the puppy. Charles reached out and put his arms around the excited puppy. "It's okay, Lily. You're okay." She climbed into his lap and licked his chin. Charles gave her a little squeeze and felt her whole tiny body shaking. Charles sniffed. He could tell that Lily had had at least one "accident" while she was in her crate. Who could blame her?

"I thought those people left," Milo said. He gave Lily a scratch behind her ears—right where her cream-colored fur was softest. "Why is she still here?" Lily climbed in Milo's lap next. She licked his chin once, and then she moved on to his nose. Milo tried to turn away, but Lily was too fast. Her little black nose and pink tongue pushed up against Milo's face. Milo could not stop laughing.

"I don't know," Charles said. "Maybe they're coming back for her."

"Hey, what's going on in here?" Jodi stood at the door, a laundry basket against her hip.

"Charles heard something in the room, so I opened it," said Milo.

"And look who we found," Charles said. Lily squirmed in Milo's arms and let out a whine. They really needed to get her outside.

Jodi shook her head. "I've been running this inn for a long time," she said. "I thought I'd seen everything. But this takes the cake."

CHAPTER FIVE

Jodi was not looking happy—but Charles had other things to worry about.

"Lily really needs to go outside," he said.

Milo put Lily in Charles's arms.

"You'll need that, too," Jodi said, pointing to a red leash hanging from the closet doorknob. "What a mess. I've had people leave books behind, or jackets. But never a puppy. What on earth are we going to do with a puppy?"

Lily let Charles snap the leash on her collar, looking up at him with her sparkly brown eyes.

What are we waiting for? Let's go!

Charles hurried out of the room with the puppy. "What are we going to do?" Charles heard Jodi say again as he went down the stairs.

Lily knew just what to do. As soon as she'd done her business in the bushes in the inn's backyard, she was ready to play. Charles ran around the yard with her, playing chase until they were both panting. As he lay under a tree, catching his breath, he heard someone calling him. "Charles!" It was the Bean, yelling his name. Oops! Charles had totally forgotten to go back to the bay. He was only supposed to be gone a few minutes, to get his swim mask. Mom and Dad must have been worried.

"Back here!" Charles called.

The Bean ran through the open gate. "Charles!" he exclaimed. "Puppy!" The Bean jumped up and down when he saw Lily. "Charles got a puppy!"

"Charles, where have you been? We were getting worried," Mom began as she came into view. Then she stopped in her tracks. She stared at Lily. "Oh! Is this why you didn't come back to the bay?"

"That's a silly question," Dad said with a laugh. "Of course it's why he didn't come back. Isn't this the puppy who was with that family yesterday?" He knelt down to pet Lily.

Charles told them everything. "I don't understand," Charles finished. "How could anybody leave a puppy like that?"

"Maybe there's been some mistake," Dad said.

Mom nodded. "Maybe they just went away for a few hours," she said.

Charles was having a lot of fun playing with Lily that afternoon, but he felt a little sad inside, too. He really couldn't understand how anyone could not want a wonderful puppy like Lily. Sure, her bark was especially loud. She liked to jump on people. And yes, she chewed stuff. And peed in the wrong places. But these were all normal puppy habits.

"All puppies need training," Lizzie said when she and Sophie put down their books for five minutes to come out and play with Lily. "Some just need a little more than others."

Charles definitely wanted to hear what Jodi found out when she called the family. He lingered around the house so he would be the first to hear it if she had any news. Dad went and got take-out sandwiches and fries from the Snack Shack. The Petersons were eating lunch on the deck when Jodi came out through the sliding door from the kitchen.

"Did you call Lily's family?" Mom asked.

"Yes, I did," Jody said. "But it wasn't good news." She shook her head. "I spoke with the mother. She said Lily loved the beach. Like, she loved it so much that they 'felt bad'"—Jodi made quote marks in the air with her fingers—"taking her back to the city. She said they live in a small apartment, and they thought Lily would be 'happier somewhere else.'" Jodi made the air quotes again. "Can you believe it? Who does that?"

Lizzie looked outraged. "But goldens are all about their people," she said. "Lily could have been happy in an apartment, as long as she got to go out a lot. Walks, trips to the park, lots of time to play with other dogs. And plenty of cuddling at home."

Mom nodded. "You're right, but that amount of attention for a dog might just be too much for some families," she said. "It's a lot of responsibility, and a lot of work."

None of it sounded like work to Charles. To him, a puppy was just part of the family. He loved playing and cuddling with Buddy, and even taking him for walks or giving him a bath could be fun.

Just then, Milo came barreling down the stairs. Lily jumped up to bark at him. She grinned a doggy grin and wagged her tail.

Oh, exciting! Here comes another friend! I'll bet he wants to play!

"What's up, pup," Milo asked, kneeling down. He ruffled Lily's ears. He stuck his nose up to Lily's, and she licked it. Then he stood up and headed for the door to the kitchen.

"What are you doing, hon?" Jodi asked.

"Just getting a snack," Milo said. He appeared in the sitting room again, holding three bananas up for his mom to see. "I'm hungry."

"Then please join us for a proper meal later. You can't just stare at your computer all day and only come down to steal snacks."

"I'm not stealing," Milo said, unpeeling a banana. "I'm borrowing." He took a huge bite.

Charles smiled. He could tell that Jodi wanted to laugh, but she hid it.

"Hey, maybe we could keep this pup," Milo said to his mom. "I mean, that is, if her first family, or Charles and his family, doesn't want her. She's pretty sweet." Milo reached down and scratched under Lily's chin. The puppy looked up at him with her big brown eyes.

Jodi's eyebrows shot up. "Are you kidding? Who would take care of her? I'm way too busy, Sophie's got her dance classes every day, and you hardly ever leave your room."

Charles thought Milo's idea was terrific. Lily could be so happy living at the inn, where she'd meet all kinds of people.

"Okay," Milo said, holding up his hands. "It was

just an idea." He took a few backward steps to the staircase. "Just an idea," he said again. When he reached the bottom step, he whipped around and raced up the stairs. "See ya!"

Jodi sighed. She turned back to Charles's parents. "Ever since his brother went to college, Milo is on his computer all the time." She sighed again. "They used to throw the football or the Frisbee, or go to town together. Now it's just video games."

Lily had curled up on Charles's lap. Charles buried his fingers in the warm, thick fur around her neck. Lily took deep, sleepy breaths. This frisky pup seemed to have two speeds: wild and crazy, or asleep.

"Well," Charles heard Mom say. "We're here until Friday. I could be wrong, but I think Charles and Lizzie will help take care of Lily."

"Yes, yes!" Charles said. He was excited, but he

tried to stay calm. Lily was so relaxed now, about to drift off for a nap.

"Sure," Lizzie said. "But—Sophie and I have a lot of things we want to do, too." She looked at her new friend, and Charles could see that she felt torn. Normally Lizzie would be one hundred percent available to help with any puppy.

"Any help would be amazing," said Jodi.

"And we can help find her a new forever home, too," Charles added.

"We're not here for that long, Charles," Dad pointed out.

"And we are on vacation," Mom reminded him, with a smile.

"I know, I know," Charles said. He had a secret hope. Maybe, by the time vacation was over, Lily would have found her forever family . . . with the Petersons.

CHAPTER SIX

"Absolutely not!" Mom said, holding her slippers high in the air. Lily sat at her feet. The puppy jumped up on Mom's legs. She stared at the slippers in Mom's hand and let out a few yips.

"You don't have to decide now," Charles said. He realized he had probably asked too soon. Mom wasn't ready to think about adopting another puppy permanently, even one as cute as Lily.

"The answer's not going to change," Mom replied. "I love Buddy, you know I do. I love having a puppy. And I love fostering puppies. But two full-time puppies is one too many. Especially if the second puppy wants to eat my slippers."

Lily sat down right at Mom's feet. She lifted her chin high in the air. Her eyes did not move off the slippers. She barked again. Mom held a finger to her lips. "Shush, Lily," she said.

"She's just teething," Charles said. "She won't need to chew on things forever. She'll outgrow it."

Dad walked over to Mom and squeezed her shoulder. He took the slippers from her hand and put them out of sight, on the dresser. "I think Miss Lily needs to go out," he said to Charles.

"I took her out first thing," Charles said.

"Let's take her for a real walk," Dad said. "Maybe to the Snack Shack, for ice cream." He laughed. "For us, I mean. Not Lily."

"Okay!" Ice cream before lunch? Charles wasn't going to say no to that. He bent down and scooped Lily into his arms. "Forget about those slippers, Lily," he said. "We're going to do something much more fun." Lily licked his cheek and wriggled in his arms. She was so fluffy! And she had that fantastic puppy smell.

Mom looked at her watch, frowning. "It's kind of early for ice cream," she said.

"It's vacation," Dad said with a shrug. "We're going to take Lily out. Lizzie and Sophie are playing with the Bean. You could take a bath."

Mom smiled. Charles could tell she liked that idea. "And then . . . maybe go on a short beach walk? I could look for some birds." Mom had been into birdwatching lately.

"Sure." Dad nodded. "Get it? Shore? Like shore birds?"

Mom smiled again, ignoring the Dad joke. "A bath and a walk, that's my idea of vacation."

Lily was excited about getting out. She ran in circles, barking loudly, as soon as she saw the leash. "*Shhhh, shhhh.* Take it easy," Charles said. He waited for her to settle down. As soon as he attached the leash to her collar, the puppy bolted toward the gate. "Whoa!" he yelled.

"This puppy is used to calling the shots," Dad said. As they walked along, Lily tugged on the leash. She wanted to be in the lead. "That family let her think she was the boss."

"It's true," said Charles. He thought about the first time he had seen Lily and how she had charged right off the porch.

"I guess they had their hands full with three kids and a puppy," Dad said.

"Our family has three kids and a puppy," Charles pointed out. "But those kids were little, and they probably didn't have much experience with dogs, like we do. They didn't know how to act around a puppy."

Dad laughed out loud. "You sound like a wise old man."

"Come on, you saw them. They all ran at Lily,

screaming and grabbing at her," Charles said. "That's too much excitement for a little pup."

Dad nodded. "I know what you mean," he said. "The family didn't know any better, so Lily didn't know any better, either."

"Exactly," Charles said. He changed his hold on the leash, making it shorter so Lily was not so far ahead. And once in a while, he just stopped walking, waited for her to ease up on the leash, and then started moving again. Sometimes dogs just had to understand that they couldn't just tow you along.

The morning sun was bright and warm. Charles was excited about ice cream this early in the day. That would never happen at home! What flavor would he get? And should he push it and ask for rainbow sprinkles?

"I wonder if Debbie and Angelo would like a new puppy," Dad said.

Debbie and Angelo were the owners of the Snack

Shack. Charles remembered them well from the last time the Petersons had been in Brisco Beach. They were so nice. Debbie took the orders at a take-out window. She always remembered everyone's favorite ice cream order. Angelo worked in the kitchen, but he always stuck his head out the window to ask questions about an order—or just to say hi.

Sure enough, Debbie remembered them, too. When they got to the Snack Shack, she peered at Lily. "Didn't your family have a puppy with you the last time you were here in town?" she asked.

"We did," Dad said with a laugh. "It's amazing that you remembered."

Charles knew that Debbie was talking about Liberty, the runaway pup the Petersons had found on the beach during their last visit.

"Well, I never forget a face, especially not a cute puppy face," Debbie replied. "This one is extra adorable."

"This is Lily. She's looking for a new home," Dad said.

"Is she now?" Debbie said.

Debbie disappeared from the order window. Dad looked at Charles and raised his eyebrows. "If Angelo and Debbie adopted her, Lily would definitely be close to the beach," he whispered.

"She would love that," Charles whispered back. Still, Charles couldn't help hoping that Mom might change her mind. Lily would be so happy with their family, even if there wasn't a beach nearby. Charles was sure Lily would like their backyard almost as much. And he knew she'd love Buddy. He could just picture them playing together, out in the yard.

"Lily. Lily, no," Dad said. "Charles, pull her away. Charles!"

Charles had been lost in a daydream about

Buddy and Lily. By the time he snapped out of it, the real Lily had been up to her puppy mischief. A box of ketchup packets had been knocked to the ground, and there were paper napkins everywhere. Lily had a wet clump of napkins in her mouth, and she was tossing her head around. She let out a pretend growl.

"Where did all this come from?" Charles asked.

"It was on the counter here," Dad said. "She must have jumped up when we weren't looking. For a small puppy she sure can get into things."

"Oops." Debbie reappeared with an ice-cream cone in her hand. She smiled and shook her head. "That's one busy puppy. It didn't take her any time to make a proper mess."

Charles was surprised. Debbie didn't sound upset at all.

"Aw, she's sweet." Angelo appeared in the

window. He was smiling at Lily. He laughed as she wrestled with the napkins.

Charles started to think maybe these two would make a good family for Lily. They were so patient and kind. Lily would need someone like that. She was young and still had a lot to learn.

"She is too cute," Debbie said. "And full of mischief. She's a perfect reminder of why we don't adopt puppies anymore. Right, Angelo?" She smiled at Dad. "We always get full-grown dogs from the shelter now."

"We go for the middle-aged mutts," Angelo said. "Like us!"

Debbie laughed. She elbowed Angelo playfully. "Don't worry about cleaning that mess up," she said to Charles. "Your ice cream is going to melt."

But Charles handed his cone to Dad. "Hold this for a minute," he said as he bent to scoop up the ketchup packets and get the napkins out of Lily's mouth. "Come on, girl," Charles said. "That's not food." Lily gave a tiny puppy snarl, showing her bright white puppy teeth as she pulled backward, tugging at the napkins.

"Oh, wow."

Charles sat back to look up. It was Milo.

"It looks like Lily's getting into trouble here, just like at the inn," Milo said.

"It's my fault," admitted Charles. "I wasn't paying attention."

"She's just a puppy," Milo said, kneeling down. "She's so quick. It only takes a second."

Charles nodded. Lily was a rascal. He thought about all the puppies they had fostered. All puppies were troublesome in one way or another, but he couldn't think of one that had been as mischievous as Lily. It might be harder than he thought to find her a new family.

CHAPTER SEVEN

Milo held out a tangle of straps. "I found this puppy harness and I thought it might help. My grandparents used to have dogs at the inn," he explained. "I found this in a closet. Your mom told me you were down here."

Milo pulled Lily into his lap and petted her as he fastened on the harness.

Dad handed back Charles's cone and went to get another for Milo. For a few minutes, Charles concentrated on his ice cream. Delicious. And Debbie had remembered that he liked rainbow sprinkles!

"A harness could be a good idea," Charles said. "It might help her stop pulling."

Lily lifted her head and licked Milo's chin. She stretched out her neck to sniff Charles's ice cream. When Dad came back with Milo's cone, she stared at him with her big brown eyes, as if she was begging for a cone of her own. Charles laughed. Lily looked so innocent! How could this puppy be such a troublemaker? Lily yawned and blinked, settling down on Milo's lap.

What's so funny? I'm a little tired, so maybe I'll take a quick nap. And after that, you can take me to the beach so we can play. Okay?

"Wow, that harness works like magic," Dad joked, as Lily closed her eyes and rested her head on her paws.

"How did you do that?" Charles asked Milo.

"It isn't me, I swear." Milo held up his hands.

Dad looked at his watch. "I should go get the

Bean," he said. "Lizzie and Sophie have been watching him for a long time now."

"Are you taking him to the beach?" Charles asked.

"Yes, to the bay again," said Dad. "Want to come?"

Charles hesitated. "I think Lily would have more fun at the big beach. That's where her old family took her."

"I'll go with you," Milo offered. "That is, if Lily ever wakes up." Milo looked down at the puppy and laughed.

Lily's cream-colored belly rose and fell as she slept. She made a soft snoring noise, and her eyebrows twitched.

"She's like a toddler," Dad said. "She wore herself out, making so much mischief. All right, then. You boys have fun at the big beach. Just be sure to check in with us after an hour or so."

After Dad left, Charles and Milo talked for a while, waiting for Lily to wake up. When she did, it was the cutest thing ever. She stretched out her front paws and yawned at the same time, her eyes still closed. Her little pink tongue and tiny sharp teeth showed. And then, an instant later, the puppy was wide awake. She hopped up on Milo's lap and gave a happy yip.

Let's go! I'm all rested and ready for the next adventure!

"I think she actually likes the harness," Charles said as they headed for the beach.

Lily was still excited. She bounded out in front of Charles and Milo, but with the harness on, she didn't tug as much at the leash. She didn't try to dart off this way and that and smell every single smell. It was a small change, but it made Charles feel optimistic. With some help, Lily could definitely grow into a well-behaved dog.

As they walked on the boardwalk through the dunes and neared the beach, the sound of the ocean grew louder. Charles heard shouts and laughter, too. He spotted a family: parents and three kids on the beach. They were chasing a giant orange beach ball, kicking it and tossing it all over the place.

Lily barked. Her bright eyes followed the ball. Her ears perked up. She wagged her tail at super speed.

That looks like so much fun! I want to do that! I want to jump! I want to play! I want that ball!

Charles and Milo stopped at the end of the boardwalk and took off their shoes. Charles held tight to Lily's leash.

Charles wondered if Lily thought those were

her people. "Do you think she remembers her old family?" Charles asked.

"*Hmm*, probably," Milo said.

"These people might remind her of them. They look like a nice family," Charles said. He still wished that Lily could come home with his family, but Mom had made that sound impossible. That meant Charles had to try to find Lily her forever home, and he only had a few days. Maybe it was worth checking these folks out. But before he could move their way, the mom of the family walked toward him.

"What a gorgeous puppy!" the woman said. "Can I pet her?"

Charles nodded and smiled.

As soon as the woman knelt down, Lily put her paws in her lap and licked her face.

"That puppy really likes you," the dad said, joining them. He smiled at Lily.

"Goldens are definitely people dogs," Milo said. He stood a couple of steps behind Charles. "And— guess what? This one is looking for a new home. What do you think? She's a fun pup."

Charles was impressed. Milo must have been thinking the same way he was, and he sure didn't waste any time. The grown-ups looked at each other for a long moment. The mom raised her eyebrows. The dad smiled. Charles bit his lip.

It didn't take long for the kids to forget their game with the beach ball and notice Lily, too. "A puppy!" they all yelled together. "A puppy!" They came running, kicking up sand and laughing.

Lily scrambled out of the mom's lap and barked. She seemed to bounce in place with each tiny *ruff, ruff, ruff.*

The kids huddled around her, reaching out to pet and tickle her.

"What's her name?" asked one of the girls.

"Is she going to bite me?" asked the other.

"Can I hold her leash?" the boy asked, hopping from foot to foot.

Suddenly, the kids all seemed much younger to Charles. Charles felt his heart sink. This family was actually a lot like Lily's first family.

"Sure you can, Grady." The dad glanced at Charles and Milo. "If it's okay with these two."

Charles swallowed. He looked at Milo. Milo shrugged and nodded.

"Okay." Charles held out the leash. The boy grabbed it. Charles showed him how to make sure the leash was not too short and not too long. "Hold on tight," Charles said.

"C'mon, girl!" The boy took off, pulling on the leash so Lily would run with him. Lily looked back at Charles for a moment. Then she trotted off with the boy, jumping up every few steps.

The boy shrieked and giggled. Lily jumped

some more, then ran forward, tugging on the leash. Charles watched it all happen. In no time, the boy let the leash get really long. "Shorten it up," he yelled.

But the boy didn't seem to hear. "What's her name?" he yelled back.

"Lily," called Charles, feeling a knot in his stomach. This wasn't going well at all.

"Lily, Lily!" The other two kids took off, yelling her name as they ran toward Grady and Lily. They yelped with joy as they caught up, and Lily jumped all over them, too.

Charles and Milo exchanged glances. This was definitely not how this was supposed to go.

"Hold on tight, Grady," the dad called.

"She's still really young," Charles said to the parents. He could tell that this whole idea was a mistake. Three young kids had been too much for Lily before—why would this family be any better for her? He didn't want to run after Lily now—that might just make her even more excited. He crossed his fingers, hoping that Grady would hold on to that leash.

"She's young, but she's really cute," the mom said.

"And she seems great with the kids," the dad said.

"It would be something different for them," the mom said. "We've never had a dog," she explained to Charles and Milo. "We've only had cats."

Charles looked at the parents. He had to explain that a puppy is not the same a kitten, not at all, and that three young kids plus a puppy might be too much to handle. But where to start? He wished Lizzie were there. He looked at Milo again, but Milo just gave him a little shrug.

Lily barked. She ran circles around Grady, and then she ran at the other kids, dragging Grady behind her. Grady tripped over the leash, fell hard onto the sand, and immediately began to wail.

"Grady!" the mom yelled. She and her husband rushed toward the kids.

"Lily!" yelled Charles. He had seen Grady let go of the leash as he fell.

"Lily!" yelled Milo.

But Lily had already dashed away. She was racing straight for the waves.

CHAPTER EIGHT

"Lily!" Charles yelled her name and jumped up and down, waving his arms. "Lily, come!" She didn't even look at him. Lily just wanted to play. The puppy ran to the water, then skidded to a stop as soon as the waves reached her paws. She nipped at the sea foam and barked at the ripples.

"Don't chase her," Charles warned Milo. "That will only make her run away. Let's try to get a little closer. Then maybe we can get her to come to us." They moved slowly toward the pup, who was still busy playing with the waves. She spotted them as they got closer, and let out a few happy yips.

This is so much fun! You should play, too! Come on! Let's play!

Charles wanted to run up and grab her, but he knew she'd only take off. Then a big wave came splashing up the beach. It whooshed up over her paws. As the wave flowed past Lily, the water reached up to the puppy's chest. Even her nose got wet! She sneezed and shook her head. The fur on her belly was dripping wet. She gave a full shake, her long ears flapping. Lily sneezed again and sat down hard.

Huh. I have to admit, that was kinda scary.

Suddenly, Lily looked tired. Charles had to get her out of there, before an even bigger wave came along. "Come on, girl," he said, kneeling down. He opened his arms. "Come on!" After a moment, the soggy little puppy stumbled over to him and let him scoop her up.

"That's a girl," Charles said, wrapping her in a hug. "Good girl, Lily." He pushed his nose into the warm fur around her neck. He felt the chilly wetness of her legs seep onto his shirt. Charles breathed in her salty-puppy smell and sighed. The mischievous pup was safe—for now.

"Great job, Charles," said Lizzie. "You knew just what to do."

Charles and his family were hanging out in the Maple room at the inn. He had just told them about what had happened at the beach. He was still buzzing with the excitement and stress of it all. Meanwhile, Lily snoozed on his lap. She'd fallen asleep as soon as he'd toweled her off. She looked so peaceful when she was sleeping! She couldn't be cuter, with her chubby belly and the soft, feathered fur on her tail. The salt water had brought out her curls, and Charles played with them as she slept.

Dad was sitting next to Charles on the couch. He put an arm around Charles's shoulder and pulled him close. "Lizzie's right. You did a great job getting Lily back safe and sound. And it sounds like you also found out that those people were not the right forever family for her."

"I kind of knew right away. The kids were all grabbing at her, and Lily started barking, really barking. Before that, she had been behaving really well," Charles said. "She's actually much better with the harness on."

Just then, there was a soft knock at the door.

Mom got up and opened it.

Milo stood there, his hands in the pockets of his hoodie. "Hey."

"Hi, Milo," Mom said. "Do you want to come in?"

"Um, yeah," he said. He ducked his head and

looked out from under his long bangs. Mom smiled. She lifted a finger to her lip and made the *shhh* sound, then pointed to the Bean, who was napping on the bed.

Milo shuffled in. He went to a lounge chair in the corner, close to Charles and Lily. He sat down on the edge. He half smiled at Charles and took a breath. "I'm really sorry," he said. "I had a feeling that family wasn't right as soon as they said they'd only ever had cats."

"That's what Charles has been saying!" Dad said. "I'm guessing that after today's episode they will be a cat family for a very long time." The Bean woke up and crawled into Dad's lap.

"Or they could get a goldfish," Lizzie said.

"Goldfish are pretty," Bean said sleepily. He made his fish face.

"Yes," Mom said, stroking his head. "Goldfish are very pretty."

Charles saw Lizzie giggle at that.

"But the mom did really like Lily," Milo said.

"Lily is very easy to like," Lizzie said, shrugging.

Charles wanted to catch Milo up to where they were now. "It just seems like little kids make Lily extra excited, like that family on the beach. And like Lily's original owners."

"Lily is still very young and golden retrievers stay puppies for a long time," Lizzie told Milo. "They're so intelligent and easy to train, but they can be lively and mischievous until they're, like, four."

"That sounds like a good thing," Milo said. "I mean, wouldn't you rather have a lively dog?"

"Sure," Lizzie agreed. "But only if the dog knows how to behave. Lily needs someone to help her understand how to be a good dog."

Milo raised his eyebrows. "That's why I came by," Milo said. "I had an idea. I know someone who might be perfect for Lily. No little kids. Lots of out-side time. He could take her to the beach every day."

Charles almost wanted to shush Milo. He knew he was trying to help, but Charles had started to think again about how great it would be if his family could keep Lily.

Mom leaned forward. "That's great, Milo," she said. "Tell us more."

Charles frowned and stopped listening. Instead, he stroked Lily's soft ears as he watched her sleep. He really did want what was best for her. The thing was, he was pretty convinced that he knew what "the best" was: a home with the Petersons.

CHAPTER NINE

It turned out that Mom and Dad both liked Milo's idea much better than Charles's. "Not gonna happen, pal," Dad said when Charles asked again if they could adopt Lily.

"And if you want to help find her a good home, remember that we only have a couple more days in Brisco Beach," Mom added. "I think it's worth checking out Milo's idea."

The next day, Milo, Charles, and Lily started out early. "It's a short walk," Milo said as they headed down the steps.

Charles looked over his shoulder at the Fair Harbor Inn. He almost laughed when he remembered how he had thought it looked haunted. Now it looked like home away from home. And had he really only known Milo for a few days? Even though the other boy was much older, Charles felt like Milo was his friend.

The more Charles thought about Milo's plan, the more he hoped it would work. Milo was taking Charles and Lily to meet the captain of the ferry boat. "His name is Rick," Milo said as they headed toward the dock. "His dog died last year, and I'm thinking Captain Rick's probably ready for a new friend by now." Milo had explained all this already to the whole family, but he seemed to know that Charles hadn't really been listening the first time. "I think that Lily will really like Captain Rick. Plus, the ferry is a fun place where she could meet lots of people. We both know how much she likes people."

Charles just nodded. When Milo talked about a

boat captain, Charles pictured an old man with a shaggy white beard and a silly hat. It wasn't exactly the type of person Charles imagined for Lily, but he would give Captain Rick a chance.

The ferry went from the bayside of Brisco Beach to the mainland. It ran several times a day. Charles could already picture Lily sitting in the front cabin of the ferry. She'd be adorable, perched in the captain's chair. But Charles was also worried that the ferry ride—and all the people—might be too much for her.

"It'll be fun," Milo told Charles. "The ferry goes to this great little dock area on the mainland. There's an amazing grilled cheese stand there. They have all kinds of extra add-ons: bacon, apples, peanut butter. *Mmmm*, those sandwiches are so good."

Charles just nodded.

"They also have a candy shop and a cart with hot pretzels if you don't like grilled cheese," Milo added.

"Oh, I like grilled cheese." Charles looked down at Lily. Her tongue hung out, and she was flashing her tiny-puppy-tooth grin. Charles realized that Lily was ready for anything. She'd probably be fine on the ferry. "My mom gave me money," he said. "Maybe we can get some candy, too." Charles was starting to feel excited about the ferry.

"There it is," Milo announced, pointing to a large boat with two levels. The bottom part had room for a couple of cars in the back. The front had lots of benches for sitting, and windows. The top level was open to the sky, and there was a glassed-in cabin. Charles was pretty sure that was where the captain must sit.

The words "BEACH BUM" were painted on the side of the ferry. "Funny name," Charles said. "Look, Lily, it's a boat. We're going on the water." He knelt next to her so he could see everything from her level. Everything looked even bigger and

busier from down there. "It's going to be fun, girl."
Lily seemed to take it all in. Her eyes were bright.
She looked up at Milo. She turned to Charles and
licked his ear.

*This looks like an adventure! And you know I
love adventures. It'll be fun to do it with my two
favorite friends.*

Milo ruffled Lily's ears. "You're up for this,
aren't you, pup?" He grinned at Charles. "She'll
love it. I'll go get our tickets."

"Check it out," Milo said when he came back a
few minutes later. "There's Captain Rick."

Charles looked for the captain type he'd imagined but didn't see him. Milo pointed at a guy
with a tan face and shaggy blond hair. "That's
Captain Rick?" Charles asked. Captain Rick did

not have a white beard or a funny hat. Actually, he reminded Charles of his gym teacher. He wore jeans, a plain white T-shirt, and a baseball cap. Just seeing him changed Charles's mind. Already he could picture Lily spending her days with this cool-looking dude: running on the beach, playing Frisbee, and, of course, riding the ferry.

"Let's talk to Captain Rick on the return trip," Milo suggested. "By then we'll know if Lily likes the ferry."

Charles already had a really good feeling about that. Lily's fluffy ears were flapping in the breeze. She sniffed the warm salt air, her nose lifted to the sky. As soon as they got onto the boat, she dropped her nose to the deck, taking in all the new smells. She jumped onto a bench and put her paws up on the railing, stretching her neck to look out at the wide-open sea.

Charles felt the motor start up with a low rumble. People came on board and went up the stairs. The ferry began to pull away from the dock.

"Hey, Lily," Milo said, petting the puppy under her chin. "Want to go upstairs?" Milo scooped Lily into his arms. He smiled at Charles. "I'll carry her so you can hold on to the railing."

If Lily was happy on the lower level of the ferry, she was bursting with joy on the top deck. The wind whipped her feathered hair as she greeted the other passengers with a wagging tail.

Soon, the ferry docked on the other side of the bay, and Milo, Charles, and Lily followed the crowds down the gangplank. Milo said they had an hour before the ferry would head back to Brisco Beach. "Let's take a walk, and then we can get some lunch," Milo said. They walked on a long wooden pier that went way out into the water. Charles held tight to Lily's leash so she couldn't chase the seagulls.

"I was pretty sure Lily would like the ferry," Milo said. "She's always up for fun. And I'm sure she'll like Captain Rick. He would definitely keep her on the go, which is what she needs." Milo bent down and gave Lily a good scratch all over her back. Lily closed her eyes. She pushed her black nose up against Milo's leg.

After their walk, they went to the snack bar for grilled cheese sandwiches. Charles got a plain one, no add-ons, and thought it was the most delicious grilled cheese he had ever eaten. Afterward, Milo held Lily's leash while Charles went to the candy store. Charles picked out gummy worms for him and Dad and malted milk balls for Lizzie and Mom. He also got a bag of jelly beans for Milo, as a thank-you for helping with Lily.

Back on the ferry, they went straight to the top deck. Charles thought he should hold Lily when they met Captain Rick. He picked her up, but

Lily squirmed in his arms. As he put her down, Captain Rick appeared from out of the cabin.

"Hey, Milo!" he said. "How's it going?"

"Great," Milo said. "Captain Rick, I want you to meet my friends. This is Charles, and this is Lily."

Captain Rick shook hands with Charles, then got down on his knees to let Lily smell his hands. She wriggled up to him, grinning and wagging her whole little butt. Captain Rick laughed. "Well, any friend of Milo's is a friend of mine. But especially the furry ones. Hi, Lily, how do you do?"

It took about two seconds for Lily to climb into Captain Rick's lap. She licked his cheek and wagged her tail.

Another new friend. This is my lucky day, for sure!

Milo and Charles looked at each other and smiled.

"Lily, I think you can tell that I like you," Captain Rick said. He threw his head back and laughed when she licked his neck. "Too bad you don't like me."

Charles laughed. He glanced at Milo. The older boy nodded. It was time to pop the question. "Actually, Lily is looking for a new home," Charles said. "I mean, Milo and I are helping to find her a good home. And you seem perfect for her."

Captain Rick started to say something, but just then, a handsome, full-grown yellow Labrador retriever walked out of the captain's cabin. The dog stepped up to Captain Rick and placed a big paw on the man's leg, right next to Lily.

CHAPTER TEN

Charles's heart fell when he saw the other dog.

"Hey, guys, meet Popeye. Pops for short." Captain Rick took one hand off Lily and rubbed Pops behind the ears. "He's my second mate these days."

Charles knew "second mate" was a boating term for the person who helped sail a ship.

"Huh," Milo said, digging his hands deep in his pockets. "I didn't know you got another dog."

"Yeah, a couple months back," Captain Rick said. "He was the first dog I met at the shelter, and I knew he would be the perfect ferry dog. I was right." Captain Rick put an arm around Pops and gave him a squeeze.

"Then I guess you're not looking for a puppy just now," Milo said.

Captain Rick shrugged. "I wouldn't mind having a puppy around, too." He gave Lily a long look. "Especially a puppy as cute as you, Lily girl." Then Captain Rick turned to Milo and Charles. "We can talk more in a bit, but I've got to get this barge headed back to Brisco Beach."

Captain Rick stood up and started calling out directions to his crew. But Pops stayed with Lily, Charles, and Milo. Lily was thrilled to have a new playmate. She nipped at Popeye's ears. She jumped up, scrabbling her paws on the older dog's back. When Pops curled up in the sun, close to the cabin door, Lily nibbled at his tail. Pops just sighed and put his head on his paws.

"Who knows?" Milo said. "Maybe having a big brother is just what Lily needs. He can show her the ropes. And they'd keep each other company while Captain Rick works."

"Yeah. It could be perfect for her," Charles agreed. He could see how happy Lily was, playing with Popeye.

Pops let out another big sigh as Lily climbed up onto his back. Lily pushed her cold nose into the bigger dog's tired face. When Pops buried his nose under his paw, Lily got bored and trotted away.

Lily was fast! Charles grabbed her leash but not before Lily had pulled a bright orange life jacket off its hook. The puppy started dragging it behind her. "Lily, no," Charles said. "Drop it." But Lily didn't listen. She shook the jacket with all her might. Lily the troublemaker was up to her old tricks!

Then Pops got to his feet. He grabbed one end of

the life jacket and tugged. The big dog pulled, his ears back. Lily tugged, too, her tiny teeth bared.

Finally! You're playing with me! See! It's so much fun!

Lily pulled with all her might, wagging her tail and letting out little puppy growls. Popeye pulled, too, but his tail did not wag at all. He growled, deep in his throat, and Charles saw his lips draw back over his big white teeth. That was not a good sign.

"Lily thinks it's a game," Charles said. "But I'm not sure Pops does."

"What should we do?" Milo asked.

"Let go, Lily," Charles said. But Lily wasn't listening to him. Charles handed her leash to Milo.

Charles inched forward slowly and reached for a corner of the life jacket. "Come on, you two.

It's no big deal. Just drop it." He kept his voice calm, but firm. Pops let go right away. "Good boy," Charles said, rubbing Popeye's silky ears.

Lily wasn't ready to quit the game. She shook her head. She tossed the jacket all around. Finally, Charles managed to calm her down and get the jacket back. "Nice work," he heard someone say. He looked up to see Captain Rick standing there. He had seen the whole thing. Charles felt his shoulders sag. He knew what Captain Rick's answer would be now.

Charles was right. Sure, Captain Rick was super nice about it, and he still gave Lily lots of attention as they said good-bye. But they all knew the truth: Pops was not ready to share his captain with another dog. "Guess I'll have to wait on that puppy idea," said Captain Rick, as he said good-bye at the pier.

Charles felt a knot in his stomach as he walked

off the ferry with Lily and Milo. Time was running out to find Lily the right home. Charles had liked Captain Rick so much. Nothing seemed to be working out.

"Maybe it isn't only the best thing for Pops," Milo said as they headed back to the Fair Harbor Inn. "I'm thinking that Lily deserves to have a family of her own, too." He kicked at a stone. "Still, she'd have loved being on that ferry every day."

Charles saw that Milo seemed pretty bummed about things not working out with Captain Rick. "Don't worry," Charles told him, as they walked up the street. "She's a good puppy. We'll find her a good home."

Milo nodded. "She's the best puppy, and she deserves the best home." He sighed. "We were so close, with Captain Rick. Sorry, Lily. I really thought that would work out."

Lily did not seem upset at all. Her tongue hung

out, and she held her tail high, wagging it happily as she trotted along just a bit in front of them.

I don't care where we're headed, as long as I'm with friends.

Charles noticed how Milo kept the leash at just the right length and didn't let Lily pull. The two of them seemed so natural together, like they'd been friends forever. Charles thought about all the ways that Milo had helped with Lily, and how well he understood her.

Suddenly, Charles knew. He knew just what he had to do.

"Should we take Lily to the beach?" Milo asked when they got to the boardwalk. "She loves it there, and maybe we can find another family for her."

"That's a great idea," said Charles. "A family with no other dog, and older kids. That's exactly what I was thinking. But you and Lily go ahead. I'll catch up with you, but first there's something I need to do back at the inn."

Milo shrugged. "Okay, see you soon. Come on, Lily," he said, "I guess it's just you and me." He and Lily took off down the boardwalk, and Charles ran back to the inn as fast as he could. There was no time to lose. In two days, the Petersons would be headed home. Could he make sure Lily had found the special home she deserved before that?

Half an hour later, Charles headed back to the beach. But this time, his whole family was with him—and so was Milo's. Sophie and Lizzie skipped along on the flat sand near the shore. The grown-ups, Mom, Dad, and Jodi, came walking behind. Charles led the way, holding the Bean's hand, pulling his little brother back whenever the Bean tried to race into the waves.

Charles spotted Milo and Lily, playing near the lifeguard stand. "Milo!" he yelled, waving his arms.

Milo looked up and waved back.

Charles let Mom take the Bean's hand so he could run ahead. "Milo, guess what?" he said when he got closer to Milo and Lily. "You'll never believe it."

Milo raised his eyebrows. "What? What's going on? Is that my mom? What's she doing here? She's always too busy to come to the beach."

Charles dropped to his knees in the sand to give Lily a hug while he caught his breath. She wriggled and yipped and climbed all over him.

Yay, you're back! Did you come to play? Please play! We can have so much fun.

Charles looked up at Milo. He couldn't wait to tell him the news. "Your mom changed her mind!" he said. "You can keep Lily! You can keep her forever!"

Milo broke into a huge grin. "What? Really? That's the best news ever!"

The rest of the group joined them: Mom and Dad, Lizzie and the Bean, Jodi and Sophie. Everyone was smiling.

Sophie squatted down and put her face up to Lily's. Lily licked her nose and Sophie giggled. "I still can't believe you're ours forever," Sophie said, putting her arms around the wriggling pup.

"I can't believe it, either," said Dad. "I never expected this."

"Neither did I, but what can I say?" Jodi asked, shrugging. "Lily just seems so at home at the inn now, like she's already part of the family. And I know Milo and Sophie will help to take on lots of the puppy chores. Right, kids?"

"Yes!" they said together.

"But, Mom," Milo said, "how—I mean when— I mean, I can't believe you changed your mind!"

He pulled Lily onto his lap and kissed the top of her head.

"Charles convinced me," Jodi said. "He pointed out that helping Lily got you out of your room and made you forget all about those silly video games. I think you just needed another friend to pal around with, after Jeremy left for college. How could I say no to that?" Jodi sat down on the sand between Sophie and Milo and put an arm around each of them. Lily, nestled in Milo's lap, grinned up at her new family.

"Everybody happy," the Bean said, reaching out to pet the puppy's soft, creamy fur.

"Yes, everybody is happy," Mom repeated.

Charles grinned at Lizzie. "Everybody's happy," he agreed. "But you know what? I think Lily is happiest of all."

PUPPY TIPS

If you plan to travel with your dog, it's important to know that he or she will be welcome wherever you go. There are many books and websites that feature dog-friendly inns and hotels. There are also plenty of parks, attractions, and even restaurants and cafes where dogs are welcome. You can help your parents research and plan a trip that will be as much fun for your pet as it is for the rest of your family. Please make sure your dog is house-trained and has learned some basic manners before you take him or her traveling, so all these places *stay* pet-friendly!

P.S. Obviously, don't leave your puppy behind somewhere no matter how troublesome he or she is! That is totally, absolutely, one-hundred-percent not okay.

Dear Reader

I've always enjoyed traveling with my dogs. It's fun for them to see, smell, and explore new places and things—and having a companion along makes everything more fun for me, too. I've taken dogs on ferry rides, to beaches and lakes, and to special hiking or skiing destinations in the mountains—anywhere I can get to by car. It takes a little extra planning to take your dog along, but it's worth it.

Yours from the Puppy Place,

Ellen Miles

HOME BASE

YOUR FAVORITE BOOKS COME TO LIFE IN A BRAND-NEW DIGITAL WORLD!

- Meet your favorite characters
- Play games
- Create your own avatar
- Chat and connect with other fans
- Make your own comics
- Discover new worlds and stories
- And more!

Start your adventure today! Download the **HOME BASE** app and scan this image to unlock exclusive rewards!

SCHOLASTIC.COM/HOMEBASE